P9-CAY-681

Pippo the Fool

Tracey E. Fern
Illustrated by Pau Estrada

Charlesbridge

"A contest! A contest!"

The news swept across the broad piazzas and twisted through the narrow streets of Florence.

"To design a dome for the cathedral," the market women whispered over their plump, purple figs.

"Bigger than any dome ever built!" the tapestry weavers rumored over their threads of wool and gold.

"Two hundred gold florins prize money!" the potters murmured over their mounds of oozing clay.

Soon the news trickled into the ears of Filippo Brunelleschi, better known in Florence as Pippo the Fool.

As soon as he heard about the contest, Pippo knew it was the chance he had been waiting for.

Pippo was a goldsmith who could twist gold into filigree as delicate as a snowflake and cut jewels so they sparkled like the sun. But instead of making beautiful trinkets, Pippo whiled away his days designing peculiar machines no one needed and sketching outlandish structures no one wanted to build. They were just too odd—just like Pippo.

"If I can win the contest," Pippo thought, "I will finally lose that nickname once and for all!"

Pippo rambled through the streets, pondering how he could build the dome.

"Pippo!" Lorenzo Ghiberti called with a smile as wide as the River Arno. "What's your hurry? Come tell me your ideas for the dome."

Pippo stopped in his tracks. Lorenzo was the most famous sculptor in Florence. He had never paid any attention to Pippo before—other than to snicker at him.

"Surely you have ideas of your own," Pippo answered. "I'm saving my ideas for the judges."

"Pippo the Fool!" Lorenzo snickered, his smile disappearing with a snap. "You live like a hermit, dress like a pauper, and smell like a pig! No one would let you build even a simple shack!"

Pippo was determined to prove Lorenzo wrong.

Building the dome had puzzled the greatest architects in Italy for more than one hundred years. What could support such an enormous dome without ruining the beauty of the cathedral? What could hold the dome up until the mortar dried? How could tons of marble be hauled from the quarry to the cathedral? And how could so much marble be hoisted so high in the sky?

"This is a job for a genius," Pippo said happily as he sat down to sketch. "Just perfect for me!"

Pippo spent weeks preparing for the contest. He sketched soaring columns and sturdy walls, graceful arches and curving domes. He calculated the exact dimensions of each window, brick, and plank. He carved stones that locked together like a jigsaw puzzle and mixed cement that could withstand earthquakes.

The longer Pippo sketched and calculated and carved, the more certain he was that he had solved the riddles of the dome in ways that none of the other contestants—not even Lorenzo—would ever dream of. Finally he was ready.

On the morning of the contest, Pippo clutched his sketch close and pushed his way through the chattering crowd into the cathedral. Silence fell as the judges swept through the doors and called forth the contestants.

Pippo stepped forward. So did a dozen master builders from all over Europe. So did Lorenzo.

"We shall listen to the contestants' ideas today and shall announce the winner in due course, when all is said and done, and," the judges said after a quick huddle, "whenever we feel like it. You may begin."

One by one, the masters presented their plans.

The master from Siena had designed a dome made of featherweight pumice. The judges raised their eyebrows. A dome made of pumice would topple in the first gusty windstorm.

The master from Pisa designed a dome that was built over a giant mountain of dirt sprinkled with coins. When the dome was done, the master hoped that the Florentines would dig the dirt away to find the coins. The judges sighed and scratched their chins. They were getting worried.

Then Lorenzo unveiled his sketch with a flourish.

"*Bellissima!*" the judges swooned. "Such beauty! Such grace!"

Then they noticed that Lorenzo's dome was propped up on towering wooden columns. The judges groaned and rubbed their foreheads.

"How will we ever collect so much timber?" the judges asked Lorenzo. "We will need to chop down all the forests of Italy!"

"You are far too important," Lorenzo said, as he flashed the judges his most charming smile, "to trouble yourselves with such small details."

"Hmmmm," the judges murmured uncertainly. "Well, it is true that we are extremely important."

Finally the judges turned to Pippo's plans. They could not believe their eyes. Surely this was the craziest idea yet! Pippo's dome seemed to float over the cathedral like a great balloon. It had no columns, no earth, no scaffolding to support it.

"How do you plan to build such a dome?" the judges asked. "What will hold it up?"

Pippo would not tell. He was worried that Lorenzo would steal his idea.

"Pippo is *pazzo!*" Lorenzo said with a laugh. "Why should a great artist such as I need his crazy ideas?"

The judges agreed. They carried Pippo out of the cathedral like a platter of pasta and dropped him in a heap in the center of the piazza.

"If the judges need proof," Pippo thought as he headed back to his workshop, "I'll give them proof! And then they will call me Pippo the Genius."

The judges spent weeks mulling over the designs of the other contestants. Meanwhile Pippo gathered cartloads of mortar and thousands of bricks. Then he began building a model of his dome.

As Pippo worked, he felt a strange little bubble percolating in his chest. "Perhaps it's exhaustion," he thought, "or a severe case of indigestion." But as Pippo's model grew, the bubble did, too, until it seemed to fill his heart, his mind, and his soul.

As he looked at his finished model, Pippo finally realized: the bubble was joy. His dome was more beautiful than any building he had ever imagined. Pippo was sure he had created a masterpiece that no one would laugh at.

By now, the judges were so discouraged with the other silly schemes, they were ready to consider the ideas of a fool.

The judges walked inside Pippo's model. Pippo had designed two domes, one tucked inside the other. The inner dome was built in rings, stacked one on top of the other. The outer dome was supported by twenty-four ribs and was cinched by sandstone and wooden chains hidden in its walls to keep it from collapsing. No one had ever seen anything like it.

Pippo had thought of every detail. He spaced seventy-two tiny holes in his dome so the wind would whistle through and not blow it down. He built a stairway between the inner and outer domes so workers could easily repair them. He attached hooks for scaffolding so murals could be painted inside. He made marble gutters to whisk rainwater off the dome. Pippo even had his friend Donatello decorate it with fancy gilded carvings.

The judges nodded and muttered. They pointed and measured. They nodded some more. They did not let out one snicker.

The judges hustled back to the cathedral to confer and nod and mutter some more. Finally they announced their verdict.

"Pippo Brunelleschi, you shall build your dome . . ."

Pippo interrupted with a great roar of joy.

". . . with the help of Lorenzo."

Pippo felt his bubble of joy explode with a thunderous POP. Work with Lorenzo! Lorenzo, who did nothing but spout insults! It was unthinkable!

Pippo stormed and shouted and stomped. The judges were not impressed. They were far more taken with Lorenzo's blinding smile.

"You will work with Lorenzo," the judges declared, "or not at all."

They left Pippo to stew.

"I shall do all of the labor," Pippo told Donatello, "and receive only half of the honor. I would truly be a fool to make such a bargain."

"But you mustn't forget your dome," Donatello reminded Pippo.

After a few days, Pippo's temper began to cool. He imagined how his dome's red bricks would glow like the setting sun. He imagined standing in the cool, dark shelter of its shadow. He imagined how it would soar over Florence like a crown. Slowly he felt the bubble begin to grow again.

"I would truly be a fool," Pippo finally realized, "to allow my pride to be bigger than my dome."

Pippo went to work.

Day after day, Pippo worked like a whirlwind. He forged chains and chiseled stones. He carved models out of turnips. He built a wagon that converted into a raft to haul marble from the quarry to the cathedral. He crafted a hoist that lifted tons of marble, brick, and mortar hundreds of feet into the air. Pippo had his hand in everything.

Lorenzo, on the other hand, did nothing useful. He sipped cappuccino. He gossiped with the market women. And of course, he snickered about Pippo the Fool.

Pippo paid no attention. By now he was too happy watching his dome rise over the cathedral to worry about Lorenzo or the market women or his nickname.

Then one day Pippo felt a bubble in his chest that was not joy—it was exhaustion. Pippo's head hurt, his back ached, and his appetite disappeared completely.

"Surely Lorenzo can take care of my dome for one day," Pippo thought as he curled up in bed.

"What shall we do today?" the workers asked Lorenzo as they milled around the cathedral. Lorenzo shrugged and tried not to look foolish.

Silence fell over the city. The blacksmiths' hammers did not ring. The oxcarts did not rumble. The forges did not belch smoke.

The judges hurried to the cathedral.

"Why don't you do something?" they asked Lorenzo as the workers wandered home.

"It's Pippo the Fool's job to handle the minor details," Lorenzo said, smiling the smile. "I cannot possibly be bothered with such trifles."

"And we can no longer be bothered with you," the judges answered. They fired Lorenzo on the spot.

As soon as Pippo heard the news about Lorenzo, he began to feel much better. His head stopped hurting, his back stopped aching, and he ate a nice veal chop, a handful of plump figs, and a wedge of cheese.

Then Pippo threw off his covers, hurried to the cathedral, and got back to work.

Summer after summer, he sweated under the molten sun, working to the rhythmic click of the cicadas.

Winter after winter, he shivered under the gray sky, working to the shrill chatter of the starlings.

Finally, sixteen years after he had begun, Pippo tapped the last brick in place.

Trumpeters and pipers blew a fanfare.
The bells of the city pealed in joy.
And Pippo was given a seat of honor
in the center of the piazza.

"Bravo!" the judges cheered.
"Your dome will bring Florence joy
for all eternity!"

"Bravo!" the tapestry weavers cheered.
"Your dome is the most magnificent in
all the world!"

"Bravo!" the market women cheered.
"Pippo the Genius!"

"*Finalmente!*" Pippo thought happily.
"A nickname perfect for me!"

Pippo's dome in the late 20th century, with the lantern he later designed on top.

Author's note

Pippo the Fool is based on a true story. Filippo Brunelleschi was born in 1377 and grew up in the shadow of Florence's Cathedral of Santa Maria del Fiore.

Pippo's father wanted him to become a notary and spend his days drafting legal documents. Pippo had other ideas. He became a goldsmith, clockmaker, sculptor, and inventor. But Pippo's true love was architecture.

Pippo designed several buildings in Florence, including the Pazzi Chapel, the Foundling Hospital, and a church known as Santo Spirito. The dome of Santa Maria del Fiore was his most difficult and spectacular project.

No one had ever attempted to build such a large dome, and no one had any idea how such a dome could support itself. Many architects believed that without bulky external buttresses, such an enormous dome would simply collapse like a house made of cards. The dome was so large that it would even buckle the temporary wooden scaffolding that was typically used to support small domes until the mortar dried.

Pippo solved these problems handily. He designed a small, strong, circular inner dome to support the weaker, eight-sided outer dome and buried chains in the domes' walls to support them invisibly. Pippo then created many differently-shaped bricks, quick-drying mortar, and a complicated, interlocking brickwork pattern to hold both the inner and outer domes together without any temporary wooden framework.

Pippo began work on the dome in 1420. More than three hundred stonecutters, masons, and other laborers worked on the dome. They used an estimated seven hundred trees and seventy million pounds of marble, brick, stone, and mortar.

The finished dome soars nearly 295 feet from the ground and took sixteen years to build. When the dome was nearly complete, Pippo competed in another contest to design a lantern for the top of the dome. He won again.

Pippo died in 1446, barely one month after the cornerstone of the lantern was laid. He was buried in a place of honor under the cathedral. His tombstone reads: "Here lies the body of the great ingenious man Filippo Brunelleschi of Florence." Pippo would have been thrilled that they finally got it right!

Illustrator's note

Illustrating *Pippo the Fool* has been a wonderful adventure. My search for inspiration and references took me back to the city of Florence, to climb to the top of the dome and to discover the work of the masters of the early Italian Renaissance. For the inquisitive reader, the illustrations contain many little clues from their work, such as a couple of monks and their donkey from Giotto, a monkey on a window from Masaccio, and a wild boar from Domenico Ghirlandaio.

The more I studied these artists, the more I marveled at their genius. After all, they produced their work in the midst of continuous warfare and strife, barely two generations after the Black Plague had decimated Europe. And if the rivalry between Pippo and Lorenzo is any indication, we can assume that these folks were a difficult lot to get along with!

We don't really know what Pippo looked like. His biographer Giorgio Vasari says that he was short, ugly, and bad-tempered. Because this is a story of a little guy who in the end triumphs against all odds, it made me think of the silent films of the 1920s, and therefore my Pippo bears some resemblance to Buster Keaton.

Lorenzo (who, incidentally, is not purposefully modeled after Gérard Depardieu) is the villain of the story, even though he was a brilliant artist and probably not as obnoxious in reality as I depicted him. Let me just say this about him: if he wears tights and shoes of different colors, it's because that was precisely the fashion of the time for those who were really cool!

The depiction of the construction of the dome is straight from my imagination, as there are no pictures from the time. I'm not an architect, so please accept my buildings with a bit of artistic leniency.

Resources

King, Ross. *Brunelleschi's Dome: How a Renaissance Genius Reinvented Architecture.* New York: Walker & Co., 2000.

Medici: Godfathers of the Renaissance. http://www.pbs.org/empires/medici/index.html

The Renaissance: Winds of Change, 1500 to 1750 AD. CD-ROM. San Francisco: Teaching for Thinking Inc., 2004.

Riddle of the Dome: Florence Cathedral and Filippo Brunelleschi. Videorecording. Princeton, NJ: Films for Humanities & Sciences, 2001.

Vasari, Giorgio: *The Lives of the Most Excellent Painters, Sculptors, and Architects.* New York: Modern Library, 2006.

Walker, Paul Robert. *The Feud that Sparked the Renaissance: How Brunelleschi and Ghiberti Changed the Art World.* New York: HarperCollins Publishers, 2002.

For Doug, Samantha, and Ali, who always encourage my own foolish pursuits—T. E. F.

For my parents, David and Frances, with love, admiration, and gratitude—P. E.

2011 First paperback edition

Published by Charlesbridge
85 Main Street
Watertown, MA 02472
(617) 926-0329
www.charlesbridge.com

Library of Congress Cataloging-in-Publication Data
Fern, Tracey E.
Pippo the Fool / Tracey E. Fern ; illustrated by Pau Estrada.
p. cm.
Summary: In fifteenth-century Florence, Italy, a contest is held to design a magnificent dome for the town's cathedral, but when Pippo the Fool claims he will win the contest, everyone laughs at him. Based on a true story.
ISBN 978-1-57091-655-7 (reinforced for library use)
ISBN 978-1-57091-793-6 (softcover)
1. Brunelleschi, Filippo, 1377-1446—Juvenile fiction. 2. Santa Maria del Fiore (Cathedral: Florence, Italy)—Juvenile fiction. {1. Brunelleschi, Filippo, 1377-1446—Fiction. 2. Santa Maria del Fiore (Cathedral: Florence, Italy)—Fiction. 3. Florence (Italy)—History—1421-1737—Fiction. 4. Italy—History—1492-1559—Fiction.} I. Estrada, Pau, ill. II. Title.
PZ7.F3589Pip 2008
{E}—dc22 2007002283

Printed in China
(hc) 10 9 8 7 6 5 4 3 2 1
(sc) 10 9 8 7 6 5 4 3 2 1

Illustrations done in watercolor and gouache on Guarro paper
Display type and text type set in P22 Mayflower
Color separations by Chroma Graphics, Singapore
Manufactured by Regent Publishing Services, Hong Kong
Printed June 2010 in Shenzhen, Guangdong, China
Production supervision by Brian G. Walker
Designed by Susan Mallory Sherman